Bantam Books in the Choose Your Own Adventure® Series
Ask your bookseller for the books you have missed

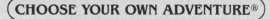

# JOURNEY TO THE YEAR 3000

## BY EDWARD PACKARD

## ILLUSTRATED BY LESLIE MORRILL

BANTAM BOOKS

TORONTO · NEW YORK · LONDON · SYDNEY · AUCKLAND

RL 5, IL age 10 and up

JOURNEY TO THE YEAR 3000
A Bantam Book / March 1987

CHOOSE YOUR OWN ADVENTURE® is a registered trademark of
Bantam Books, Inc. Registered in U.S. Patent and Trademark
Office and elsewhere.
Original conception of Edward Packard.

ISBN 0-553-26157-6

Published simultaneously in the United States and Canada

Bantam Books are published by Bantam Books, Inc. Its trademark, consisting of the words "Bantam Books" and the por-
trayal of a rooster, is Registered in U.S. Patent and Trademark
Office and in other countries. Marca Registrada. Bantam
Books Inc., 666 Fifth Avenue, New York, New York 10103.

PRINTED IN THE UNITED STATES OF AMERICA

O      09876543

Dear Reader;

I think you'll agree with me, after reading it, that *Journey to the Year 3000* is a *super adventure.* Not only is it a good deal bigger than a regular Choose Your Own Adventure book, but I believe you'll find it to be one of the most exciting and dangerous adventures you've ever had. You will find yourself pitted against Styx Mori, the greatest tyrant Earth has ever known. The odds against you are enormous. If you trust to luck, your chances of overcoming Styx Mori and saving Earth are only one in two hundred fifty-six thousand. But with skill, daring, and determination—and intelligence—you *can* succeed.

I'm betting you'll enjoy this book, and I wish you much good luck and good fun.

Edward Packard

# WARNING!!!

Do not read this book straight through from beginning to end. These pages contain many different adventures you may have as you journey to the year 3000. From time to time, as you read along, you will be asked to make decisions and choices. Your choices may lead to success or disaster.

Your adventures are the result of your choices. *You* are responsible because *you* choose! After you make your choice, follow the instructions to see what happens next.

Think carefully before you make a move. In the year 3000 the most abhorrent tyrant in history rules the solar system. Only you can vanquish him!

"Would you like to take a trip to the year 3000?"

The person who asks you this question is not just one of your teachers or friends, but your next-door neighbor, Dr. Irene Grambling. She happens to be a very brilliant scientist who works on secret government projects.

"Why not?" you say with a smile.

"I'm serious," Dr. Grambling answers. She's a large, slightly plump woman who looks friendly when she's smiling, and very stern when she's not. When she says she's serious, she means it!

Your eyes widen. "Do you mean you have a time machine?"

"Not quite," Dr. Grambling says. "It will be several hundred years before we can invent anything that sophisticated. I have something in mind that's a lot simpler."

"What can that be?"

"A computerized self-propelled orbiting space capsule in which the occupant goes into hibernation for approximately one thousand years."

"And you mean I could be the one who tries it?" You're practically shaking with excitement, or fear, you can't be sure which!

"Normally," Dr. Grambling continues, "an astronaut would be selected for this project, but the hibernation technique works only on people who aren't fully grown. I've recommended you for it because you're the right age, because you're intelligent, because you're resourceful, because you're courageous, and because you love adventure."

*Turn to page 2.*

"It sounds like more than an ordinary adventure," you say. "It sounds like a *super adventure*."

"I think it will be," Dr. Grambling agrees.

"But . . . how will I get back to the present?"

"Good question. When you asked about time machines, I said they wouldn't be invented for several hundred years. Well, by the year 3000 they should be pretty well perfected. And—I can't absolutely promise you—but if all goes well, you'll be able to get back to the present and no one will even have missed you. To everyone else it will seem as if you've never been away!"

You take a few minutes to think over Dr. Grambling's offer. She has your number all right. You *do* love adventure, and this one looks too good to miss!

*Turn to page 153.*

Two small rocket bursts are all it takes to flip your capsule out of sun orbit and send it streaking toward Mars. For the next two days you wriggle and squirm and stretch, feeling like a butterfly still locked in its cocoon. Through the window you watch a bright red star grow increasingly brighter until it becomes a disk that expands in size as your capsule approaches it. Suddenly you're pressed against the wall. The capsule is decelerating rapidly.

"Entering Mars orbit," Winston announces.

You look down eagerly at the great craters, escarpments, and canyons, and vast stretches of flat, rocky desert. There's no sign of life. The scene is more desolate than space itself. Then, as your capsule enters the planet's shadow you are plunged into darkness. The cold, forbidding surface of Mars is invisible. There are no lights—only utter blackness.

"Maybe we should leave here and try to land on Earth, Winston."

"Impossible," the computer replies at once. "There's not enough fuel."

*Turn to page 6.*

You're now wide-awake and getting really excited. And what a relief to get Winston's report that everything's working perfectly—including you!

"Thanks, Winston," you say, after sipping some rehydrated orange juice through a plastic tube. You glance through the window at the stars. Some of the constellations have changed their shape a little over the past thousand years, but they're the same friendly stars you remember—except for one that is far brighter than the others and a fainter one beside it. You guess they are not stars at all, but the earth and the moon.

"Set us on course to Earth, Winston," you say confidently. "And land in the best place possible."

You expect to hear the capsule's small maneuvering rockets going into action instantly, but instead, all is quiet.

"Winston." You try to keep the nervousness out of your voice. "Did you understand the command I just gave?"

"Of course," the computer replies. "I told you I was functioning perfectly. It's just that I'm programmed not to set course until I've found the right place to land."

*Go on to the next page.*

"Well, haven't you done that by now?" you say with some irritation. "After all, you've had over a thousand years—"

"The problem," Winston interrupts, "is that there *is* no right place to land. I'm sorry to tell you this, but Earth is entirely controlled by Styx Mori, the most ruthless, cruel tyrant in history. His agents are working everywhere—even on other planets! No matter where we land, it's almost certain you would be captured, tortured, and killed."

*Turn to page 160.*

An hour later you enter the daylight zone once again. This time your orbit is taking you closer to the planet's equator. You close your eyes and imagine that when you open them you'll see a lake or a meadow. Maybe Winston can find something with his high-resolution optical scanners.

Another hour passes. Then like a black veil drawn across your face, darkness descends again. You bury your head in your arms. More from depression than fatigue, you soon fall asleep.

The sun—still brilliant, though noticeably smaller than the sun you're used to seeing on Earth—shines in your eyes as the capsule once again enters the daylight zone. And again you look down at barren, desolate landscape.

*Turn to page 12.*

"Winston, can't you find a better place?"

"I'll do my best," Winston says as the capsule shifts to a more southerly course, "but I don't think you're making the right decision."

Those are Winston's last words. His feeder circuit fails exactly at the time he predicted.

You've said your last words too. There's no one to talk to as your capsule maintains its new course and speed, orbiting Mars every three hours, twelve minutes, and twenty-six seconds, year after year after year.

## The End

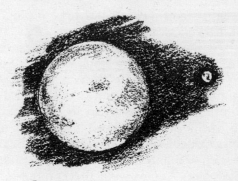

# 8

"I want to go home," you tell Winston. "I'll take my chances with the tyrant Styx Mori. Set course for Earth and land in the safest part of the United States."

"You mean what used to be the United States," Winston says. "That's the worst place on Earth to go, because it's there—in what a thousand years ago used to be a nice little town named Lolita, Colorado—that Styx Mori directs his armies of oppression."

"I don't care," you say. "I want to go home."

"Very well," Winston replies.

The rockets fire and the space capsule accelerates toward Earth.

You are tired from the excitement of waking up and then learning the terrible news about Earth, and you sleep most of the time during the trip. You're awakened from a sound sleep by Winston's warning that you're about to enter the earth's atmosphere. Performing flawlessly, the capsule descends through a heavy bank of clouds and lands on a meadow in the shadow of beautiful forested mountains flecked with snow. Your heart leaps with excitement and happiness for a moment. Then you see two air cars, bristling with laser cannons, converging on your space capsule.

"Winston," you yell at the computer, "Get us out of here!"

"Sorry," Winston says. "We wouldn't have a chance."

*Turn to page 23.*

"Let's land near that bubble dome, Winston," you say.

"Will comply," your computer answers. "Assume entry position."

Suddenly the capsule veers sharply. "Hostile fire!" Winston announces. "It's an Earth commando base, all right."

"What will we do?" you ask.

Winston is silent for a moment. Then he replies, "Computer failure imminent—we'll have to land at another location on the high plateau."

Your space capsule plunges through the thin Martian atmosphere. Only in the last few minutes of descent are you able to look around. As far as you can see in all directions there's nothing but flat red desert strewn with countless rocks of all sizes and shapes.

"I'm sorry about my failure," Winston says. "We're stuck here, I'm afraid."

*Turn to page 30.*

That night you sleep soundly. Winston wakes you with his usual cheerful voice. "Prepare to enter Earth orbit."

"Can't we land? Surely things aren't so bad on Earth as you think."

"I'm afraid they are," Winston replies, "as you can observe through the starboard window."

Two rockets are streaking toward you.

"Winston!"

"They're Styx Mori's defense missiles."

"But he doesn't need to defend himself against me!"

Winston does not reply, and in the second remaining you realize it's because he doesn't have time to finish his sentence. There was no point in beginning it.

Winston was so logical.

### The End

"Emergency!" Winston suddenly announces. "We must land immediately! There's an eighty-seven-percent probability that my main feeder circuit will fail in twenty-three minutes and fourteen seconds. I've found two possible landing sites. One of them is an extremely deep canyon at twenty degrees south latitude. I register an unusually high oxygen and moisture reading there. The other site is on the Sagan Plateau, where my sensors have spotted what may be a bubble dome erected by intelligent creatures. It's so open and visible, I must conclude it's a commando base of the tyrant Styx Mori."

"Should we look for better places, Winston?" you ask.

"We-don't-have-time!" Winston's speech has speeded up! "We-can-land-at-either-of-the-sites-if-you-select-one-within-thirty-seven-seconds."

At that moment a digital display flashes SECONDS REMAINING: *36 — 35 — 34 —*

You've got to decide now!

---

*If you decide to take a chance the feeder circuit won't fail and order Winston to look for a better place, turn to page 7.*

*If you order Winston to land near the bubble dome, turn to page 9.*

*If you order him to land in the canyon, turn to page 14.*

It seems as if you've had only half a night's sleep when you're awakened by your computer: "Entering the atmosphere of Venus," Winston says. You hear a soft *whoosh*. The first retro-rockets have fired. The capsule has already begun to decelerate.

"It's time to select a landing site," Winston says. "We've used nearly all our fuel; once we set down, we won't be able to take off again. Shall we land at the north pole, at the equator, or halfway in between?"

*If you tell Winston to land at the north pole,*
*turn to page 18.*

*If you tell him to land halfway in between,*
*turn to page 20.*

*If you tell him to land at the equator,*
*turn to page 31.*

The capsule instantly drops out of orbit. In the thin atmosphere and light gravity of Mars, heat shields aren't necessary. The descent is so swift that you have no time to study the landscape rushing toward you. All you notice is a vast plateau strewn with red boulders and a great canyon so deep that the bottom is shrouded in darkness.

In a few minutes you're floating between the canyon walls. The capsule shifts course as the canyon bends, so that now the sun is shining directly on the canyon floor. On Earth you'd probably see the river that cut the canyon walls over millions of years, but here on Mars that work was completed eons ago. The canyon floor is nothing but dry red sand and rock.

Winston cuts all power except for the minimal-thrust landing rockets, which fire with amazing precision, setting you down gently. But instead of looking out the porthole, you fasten your eyes on the numbers changing on Winston's display screen: SECONDS REMAINING TO FEEDER CIRCUIT FAILURE: 15—14—13—. . . .

Hoping against hope is not enough. Within the minute you know the worst has happened. Winston is dead, and there is no way you can get airborne without him.

You saw no signs of life as you came in for a landing. Your food supply looks as if it will last only a couple of weeks. And now that you're out of hibernation, you're using oxygen at a tremendously increased rate. Without Winston you have no way of knowing how long it will last.

*Turn to page 144.*

You direct Winston to take you to Venus. It's a two-day trip, he tells you, which is annoying because you're feeling cramped and restless after being cooped up for a thousand years.

Despite its length the trip is fascinating. The stars and planets shine brilliantly in all directions, and the view of Earth is spectacular. On the morning of the second day your home planet is less than a million miles away. Near it you can see a tiny yellow crescent—the moon.

As you streak on toward Venus you feel sad and angry. There have always been wars and cruelty on Earth, but it's horrible to think that the entire planet is now controlled by a ruthless tyrant.

By the time you're ready for a sleep period, Earth looks like no more than a brilliant star, while ahead of you Venus has swelled into a crescent of blue-green light. You close your eyes and drift off to sleep.

*Turn to page 13.*

# 16

You're afraid that the logjam will break, and your space capsule will be carried downstream and smashed in the rapids. You strap on your backpack, open the door, and start walking along a huge fallen log that extends all the way to the riverbank. As you cautiously make your way, barely able to see through the driving torrents of rain, you feel wavelets lapping at your feet. The water is rising rapidly. You keep moving, step by step. A fierce wind gusts in your face. You're halfway there now, but the footing is getting slippery—there must have been a mossy growth on this part of the log. A wave washes over your ankles. You try to move more quickly. Another gust hits. You struggle to keep your balance. A branch, riding the crest of a wave, smacks into your legs, knocking them out from under you, toppling you into the raging river! You thrash wildly, struggling to keep your head above water as the river sweeps you violently downstream. Twirling, twisting, you bob in the churning waters until the torrent brutally smashes your head into a rock.

**The End**

Since Venus is only about two thirds of the distance to the sun that Earth is, it's not hard to figure out that it will be a good deal hotter. Just looking at the size of the sun from here is enough to make you start sweating. The only places cool enough to sustain life may be near the poles.

"Try to find a good landing place near the north pole," you tell Winston.

Winston performs flawlessly, and your capsule makes a smooth entry into the Venutian atmosphere. As soon as the g-force subsides, you peer through the window, eager to get your first look at the surface of Venus. Winston informs you that a thousand years ago you would have seen a burning desert—if you could have seen anything through the thick poisonous clouds that surrounded the planet. But releasing the vast reservoirs of water from under the Venutian crust and blowing off most of the atmosphere were the greatest engineering feats of the past millennium. And now, as you can finally see, the area around the north pole is an ocean, though very different from the Arctic Ocean.

*Go on to the next page.*

The north pole on Earth is covered with ice and snow all year round, but here on Venus there is only shining blue water. Not completely water, thank goodness; Winston is zeroing you in on a small island. It looks like a desert island, but you can make out some scrubby vegetation and some fairly tall, willowy trees.

A warning buzzer sounds. "Prepare for landing," the computer says.

You brace yourself as you hear the gentle firing of the retro-rockets. Six minutes later you are safely on the ground.

*Turn to page 32.*

"Land in the middle latitude," you tell Winston. "That's where I think we're most likely to find refugees from Earth."

You brace yourself as the capsule screams through the Venutian atmosphere. After the main retros have fired and the acute deceleration phase is over, you sit up and look out. You're descending into a rain forest. You can see a fast-flowing river cutting its path through the jungle. The water is a brownish green, except in some stretches where it's almost white. Rapids, you think. Where will the capsule land? You're afraid to look as the treetops fly by. . . .

*Splash!* The capsule has landed right in the river!

"Winston!" you yell.

"Don't be alarmed," your computer announces. "We landed in the only safe place."

You look anxiously out the porthole. The capsule is drifting toward a logjam. You should be able to get to shore without even getting wet. But as the capsule comes to rest the sky suddenly grows dark. Within seconds the rain is coming down in torrents, harder than you ever saw on Earth.

*Go on to the next page.*

"Winston, if this keeps up, the river may flood. What shall I do?"

Nothing but silence.

"Winston, did you hear me?"

"Yes, I did," your computer replies at last, "but I have insufficient data."

You feel like kicking this computer. It's dumped you in a Venutian river, and now you're in danger of drowning. You gaze out the window. The rain is still streaming down. You might as well be sitting under Niagara Falls! Fortunately you seem safe for the moment. The surging water is pushing you higher up onto the logjam.

*If you get out of the space capsule, turn to page 16.*

*If you stay in the capsule and wait for the rain to stop, turn to page 29.*

The moment you wake up, you know you're in prison.

*If you've been in Earth prison before, turn to page 46; if not, read on. . . .*

What else can this tiny cell be—with plaster cracking off its walls and ceiling, a rough concrete floor, no windows, and a single door barred like an animal cage? When you look out the door, you see a long corridor lined with chipped white tile and lit by glaring neon bulbs.

"So you're awake!" An oily-skinned guard has appeared at your door.

"Let me out," you plead. "I've committed no crime."

The guard unlocks the door and steps closer. He looks at you curiously, as if you were a rare animal brought to the zoo. "You shouldn't complain. You're better off than most prisoners," he says. "No soldiers will beat you tonight, and you'll actually get something to eat for breakfast." He leans closer. "In fact, you're an honored guest. Supreme Emperor of Earth Styx Mori has asked to see you. He wants to know all about you."

The guard slaps a blindfold over your eyes and yanks you to your feet. "Come!"

*Turn to page 27.*

"Winston, put me back into hibernation for a couple of hundred years and wake me up if the situation improves."

You lie back and try to sleep, but you're all keyed up. You feel like running and jumping. After a thousand years you're really slept out!

"Come on, Winston, start the hibernation process."

The minutes tick by.

"Winston!"

Finally your computer responds. "Excuse me for the delay"—the friendly voice comes out of the speaker—"I wasn't programmed to put you back into hibernation. I had to switch to my artificial intelligence unit."

"Well, are you ready now?"

"I'm afraid there's no way to do it," says Winston. "We have no more induction enzyme on board. Besides, it would be risky to your health. Your body needs several months of normal activity before going into hibernation again."

"Winston," you say. "Could you please put us in Earth orbit? I'd just like to look over my old home planet before deciding what to do."

"We're on our way," is the reply. In less than a second you feel the restraining belts holding you down, then your weight increasing rapidly as the rockets fire.

Your space capsule streaks toward a thin blue-white crescent—Earth as it always appears when it is almost between the observer and the sun.

*Turn to page 11.*

As you carefully make your way down the steep slope of the tunnel, you are astounded to see that it ends in a descending staircase. The stone steps are square and level. You feel sure they were shaped by human hands!

As best as you can tell in the dim light, the distance between steps increases beginning a few steps farther down. To descend farther you'll have to jump down from step to step. You wonder whether you could ever get back up again.

*If you start jumping down from step to step, turn to page 33.*

*If you turn back, turn to page 76.*

The note surely means red fruit must be avoided. Your only hope lies with the nuts. You try one—it's delicious. You eat another and another. What a fantastic taste: fruity, crunchy, a little sweet, but not too sweet. The taste reminds you of chocolate, but isn't chocolate; in fact, it's better than chocolate!

As the days pass you find that you're surviving very well on the strange green nuts. But of course, you feel lonely. Apart from a few seabirds and ugly little crablike creatures that eat pieces of red fruit that have fallen to the ground, you are terribly alone. You spend much of your time peering around the horizon, hoping to see land, or a ship, or a whale, or anything but the endless blue sea. Another thing troubles you: Each day the sun drops lower and lower, closer to the horizon. Winter must be coming, and you have no idea what it will be like.

You know that if you could travel far enough over water, you'd eventually reach land. Maybe you should inflate the raft, rig up some kind of sail from the tarpaulin you found in the dugout, and set out to sea. On the other hand, it looks as if you can live indefinitely on the island. If you wait long enough, explorers—maybe refugees from Earth—will arrive.

---

*If you set out to sea in the raft,*
*turn to page 67.*

*If you decide to stay on the island,*
*turn to page 128.*

As you're led along you try to get some sense of where you're going—how many floors an elevator has taken you, how far you've been dragged across moving platforms, what voices you've heard, how many checkpoints you've passed. But as time passes you lose all sense of direction, you know only that you're in some enormous, heavily guarded building.

Finally you hear a door shut behind you. The guards strap you in a chair. Your blindfold is removed. You blink in the glare of bright lights overhead. The room is octagonal in shape, and the eight walls are faced with wood paneling. The windows are set like skylights into the high, slanted ceiling. You try to shift position to avoid the floodlight shining on you. Squinting and shielding your eyes with one hand, you look at the four huge guards standing on each side of you. Even if you had the strength of a gorilla, you would not be able to take more than a step or two toward the slim, bald man seated ten feet away on a diamond-studded throne. Three guards are positioned on each side of him, their laser pistols drawn and pointed right at you.

*Turn to page 34.*

Having decided to sit out the storm, you watch anxiously as the water continues to rise. In a few minutes the route to shore is blocked by the swirling waters. The only thing holding your space capsule against the torrent is a huge fallen tree, wedged in the logjam.

Then, as suddenly as it started, the rain stops. In a few moments the sun is shining. What a relief! For the first time you can see around you. The jungle looks more beautiful than frightening. Huge broad-leafed trees dominate the landscape. The forest floor is a bed of dead leaves and ferns, interrupted here and there by clumps of silky grass festooned with violet and pink flowers. You'd like to go ashore, but you'll have to wait until the water level falls. You sit by the window, waiting.

Instead of dropping, the water level continues to rise. How can this be? you wonder. Then you realize that, although the rain has stopped, feeder streams are still pouring their swollen contents into the river. A few minutes later your worst fears are realized. The logjam breaks, and suddenly your capsule is careening down the river, bouncing off rocks as colliding waves toss it about. You reach for your restraining straps.

*Bwong!* The capsule bounces off a rock. You are thrown violently forward. Your head hits Winston's control panel, and you're out cold.

*Turn to page 56.*

You're so depressed by this news, you don't even reply. The scene outside looks very bleak, but if you're going to go out and look around, you better hurry—the shrunken Martian sun is sinking toward the horizon. Cautiously you begin to open the hatch. You're almost blown out in the rush of air as the cabin depressurizes! You struggle to breathe the thin cold Martian air. You have survival gear, but you're not equipped for this! To travel on the plateau you'd need constant oxygen; your supply would be gone within a few days. But a far worse problem is the cold! Your nose must already be frozen.

"What's the temperature out?" you ask Winston.

"Forty below, Celsius, forty below, Fahrenheit," is the answer.

Trapped in a downed space capsule at forty below, and the sun is still shining: You don't have to ask Winston—you know it's only a matter of time until you're frozen solid.

**The End**

Figuring survival will be easier in the tropics, you instruct Winston to land near the equator. The capsule flashes through the thick Venutian atmosphere. All systems are working perfectly, and the computer-controlled rockets set you down gently as a feather.

But even as the capsule is completing its descent, you realize you've made a horrible mistake. Instead of the lush greenery you expected to find, there is nothing but drifting, blowing sand wherever you look—sand and heat. Your insulated capsule is heating up even as you strike the ground. Venus has cooled down a lot, but it's still a lot warmer than Earth. You start to open the escape hatch, but you're driven back by a blast of hot air. The outdoor temperature gauge reads seventy-six degrees on the Celsius scale—167 degrees Fahrenheit—almost hot enough to boil your blood!

You would have been just as well off landing on the sun. Even better off. At least there, death would have come quickly.

## The End

**32**

As you step out of the capsule you immediately feel pressure on your ears. You swallow and yawn, trying to adjust to the heavy atmosphere of Venus. Venus is slightly smaller than Earth, and you'd expected to feel a bit lighter here, but you can't really tell any difference.

The air smells sweet and pure except for a slight odor that reminds you of charcoal or mesquite. What you see around you looks very much like a tropical island on Earth. The huge sun hangs low over the ocean. Though it never rises high in the sky at this latitude, it still gives off lots of heat. Right now the temperature feels about eighty-five degrees—you wish you could strip off your space suit. At the north pole on Venus all you need is shorts and a T-shirt!

*Turn to page 36.*

You jump down. Suddenly your footing gives way; you slide in a cascade of crumbling rocks all the way to the bottom of the steps. You pick yourself up and look around. You've landed on the floor of a subterranean cavern. When you look back, you see you'd have to jump at least seven feet to get back to where you were!

*BWARRARRQ. BWRRR . . . RRRQ.* A sound like nothing you've ever heard echoes against the cavern walls. A smooth white object—it looks like a giant clam—rises out of the rubble around you. *Smack!* Its hinged shells close like snapping jaws on a large rock. *Smack!* It strikes again. You shrink back. Whatever this creature is, it doesn't come from Earth: Whereas all life on Earth is based on carbon, this rock monster must be made of silicon.

But there's no time to think. It twists toward you—it thinks you're a rock, and its giant shells are about to close on your body! You look up at the bottom step, seven feet above you. Can you jump that high? If you don't make it, you'll fall back into the rock monster's waiting jaws!

*If you try to jump to the step above,
turn to page 49.*

*If you run into the cavern, turn to page 148.*

So this is Styx Mori, Supreme Emperor of Earth, you tell yourself. Some of the tension leaves your body. In a way the tyrant looks more laughable than fearsome. You suspect that, like all despots, he is afraid of the very people he oppresses and must constantly act in ways that make him seem more important both to himself and his slavish admirers.

"*So!*" You are jerked up in your chair by this one sharp word. Styx Mori has spoken, but now he is silent. A wave of fear sweeps over you. What does he mean? What does he want?

Suddenly he bursts out laughing. It's the coldest, cruelest laugh you've ever heard. You sense the cause of it: Mori has seen fear in your eyes.

"Tell me everything!" he commands.

*Turn to page 38.*

Though you've landed safely, you still have to worry about finding food. As far as you can tell, the island is deserted. You climb up the beach and head for the highest ground, looking for edible plants or animals, or anything else that may give hope of survival.

Along the way you see some bright red fruit—sort of pear-shaped—growing on low scrubby trees along the way. You pick one and stick it in your pocket, wondering whether it's nutritious or poisonous. A ways farther you find other scrub trees with green nuts growing in clusters at the end of each branch. Then, when you reach the rocky ledge that marks the island's summit, you make a major discovery: a battered wooden door set into the rock. It's like a slanted cellar door of a sort you remember back on Earth.

*Turn to page 158.*

Hunched over, because the tunnel isn't high enough for you to stand up straight, you work your way through the narrow twisting passage. You don't hear the sound again, but you notice a strange odor, a sort of sweet, musty smell like nothing you remember from Earth. Something tells you that you'd better turn back—but too late! You get only a glimpse of the great lizard-face, the monstrous jaws, the rapier tongue, strong as steel and sharp as a lance, that flashes from its mouth and slices into your heart.

**The End**

In a halting, shaking voice, you tell your story, or at least the part of it you think Mori should hear. The tyrant listens. His face is like carved stone. When you are finished, he shouts, *"Enough!"*

In an instant you feel the blindfold tightening around your scalp. The guards lead you roughly out of the room. You start to cry out—you want to beg Mori to listen to you. But there's something about his eyes, something about his voice, that tells you his heart is closed.

*Turn to page 46*.

That night you sleep on a cot in a large room along with twelve other refugees. The walls are lined with huge photographs of Earth and Mars. Along one wall is a photo of the Pacific Ocean taken from space. You're fascinated by the beautiful patterns of puffy white clouds—a scene you'll never see on Mars. You drift off to sleep, dreaming of Earth.

In the morning you have a breakfast of Martian wheat and cocao milk, both made from plants that never existed on Earth when you lived there. (They are one of a few genetically engineered plants that were created especially for the peculiar conditions on Mars.) Then, with a party of ten other pioneers, you prepare for the long trek along the canyon floor, bound for the secret colony.

*Turn to page 51.*

The red fruit looks interesting to you and it tastes interesting too, sort of like a cross between pineapple and smoked salmon. It's kind of weird—you'd never eat something like this on Earth—but you've got to expect food will taste different here on Venus. You just hope the fruit is nutritious.

You take two or three more bites and then reach for some nuts to see what they're like. But as you stand up you feel as if a battering ram is smashing into your gut. A second later you double up like a jackknife snapped shut for good.

**The End**

You look up nervously at the red-tinted sky. A thin, wispy cloud is passing overhead. You're glad there's at least some variety in the Martian sky.

"How many people live in the colony?" you ask Nachim.

"Hundreds," he answers. "It's all underground. Martian animals—wehaws—live there too. They look like huge wolves and they have sharp teeth, but they're very gentle and let you ride on their backs."

"It's hard to believe they're not dangerous—with those big teeth," you say.

"Well, they need powerful jaws to bite off the crystal shards that grow in the caves. It's their only food."

"Time to get moving again," the leader calls.

"Let's go," says Nachim.

Throughout the afternoon your trudge along behind the others, excited to see the secret colony but also sad to think that you'll probably never see Earth again.

*Turn to page 48.*

Determined not to sacrifice ninety-seven innocent people just to save your own skin, you think
fast. You tell Grufurd that you climbed a trail from
the canyon floor, where your space capsule
landed, and then explain that you've spent most of
the past thousand years in hibernation.

Grufurd is suspicious. He insists you prove
you're not lying about the space capsule. With
great luck, you succeed in finding a path down into
the canyon and are able to lead Mori's commandos to the capsule.

Grufurd leaps in the air with excitement. "Styx
Mori, Emperor of the Earth, will be eager to see
this! It will distract him from thinking about how
few refugees we were able to find and kill." He
looks at you thoughtfully. "We will bring you back
to Earth along with the capsule. Styx Mori will
want to see you." Laughing, he adds, "After all,
you're a curiosity from the distant past."

Two days later you're in the commandos' spaceship headed for Earth, but you realize you're not
going to enjoy the view. A medic is standing over
you with a hypodermic syringe in his hand.

"My orders are to put you to sleep until we
arrive on Earth so you won't give us any trouble."

You start to protest, but faster than you can react, the long steel needle enters your flesh.

*Turn to page 23.*

You trudge along the canyon floor on what was once a Martian riverbed. It looks as if it's been dry for millions of years. From time to time you look up at the towering canyon walls. Though Mars is a much smaller planet than Earth, some of its features dwarf those of your home planet. This canyon must be far larger than the Grand Canyon. You estimate it's at least a three-mile vertical rise to the surrounding land, and from your perspective you can't tell whether the highest point is the canyon rim or just a setback. The air down here is denser and warmer than on the surface; that's why you have some hope of staying alive for a while without freezing or using all your oxygen. It's also the reason you hope to find a human settlement.

As you trek on, mile after mile, you begin to lose that hope. You're able to move at a fast clip, easily leaping over boulders you'd have to climb around on Earth, but the barrenness of the landscape, the absence of any sign of life, weighs heavily on your spirits.

The undersized sun is sinking in the west. The canyon floor is now cast into deep shadow, and the temperature is falling rapidly. You shudder to think how cold the night will be—too cold, you know, for you to survive.

*Go on to the next page.*

Luckily, you remind yourself, there's no wind down here. That would make it feel even colder. The absence of any breeze contributes to the absolute silence. When you stop to rest, it's so quiet you can hear the beating of your heart and the thin Martian air flowing in and out of your lungs.

You run for a while, as much for variety and to lift your spirits as to cover ground. Now it hardly seems to matter how far you go, because you've almost given up hope. Exhausted, you stop, panting for air. It is then that you hear a very faint noise up ahead around the bend in the riverbed. It sounds like running water. It must be! You break into a run.

*Turn to page 140.*

Once again you find yourself in a detention cell. A swarthy, stocky man—Colonel Gortal—stands before you. You shudder with fear as he straps electrical wires onto your body.

*"Stop shaking!"* Gortal shrieks. "You're the luckiest person alive. The Emperor likes you." He pulls the wires tight and plugs them into an electronic console. "This machine has been proven very effective. If you lie, it electrocutes you." He bursts into hearty laughter. "Now, answer this: What other planets have you been to besides Earth?"

*If you say, "Just Mars," turn to page 61.*

*If you say, "Just Venus," turn to page 102.*

*If you say, "Both Venus and Mars," turn to page 75.*

*If you say, "Just Earth," turn to page 102.*

The Martian sun has slipped behind the mountains. Darkness falls quickly here at the bottom of the canyon, and with it comes a chill that makes it seem as if you've suddenly been transported from a California desert to the arctic wastes. The leader calls for everyone to stop.

"What does this mean, Nachim?" you say. "We'll freeze if we can't find the colony before dark."

Nachim lays a hand on your shoulder. "Watch."

Suddenly part of the rock wall slides open like a huge door. A soft blue-green light shows through. An elderly man with white hair, a round face, and sparkling eyes appears at the opening.

"Welcome to Oasis, friends!"

A cheer goes up, and the band of pioneers rushes inside. You're one of the first! Ahead of you is your new home. It looks like a jungle! Lush trees and plants are growing everywhere. Cascades of water flow out of springs in the cavern walls. A brilliant light set high on the roof of the cavern serves as an artificial sun. A gurgling brook runs through the forest. Brightly colored birds sing and chirp as they flutter from branch to branch.

"It's beautiful, Nachim."

"The birds, the seeds that grew into these trees, the ferns, the artificial sun—almost everything you see—was brought here from Earth by settlers hundreds of years ago," he says. "It is our good fortune that the tyrant has never found this refuge."

*Turn to page 59.*

You leap up and grab the ledge formed by the step above and pull yourself up. It was easy! You'd almost forgotten that although Mars is a cold, barren, oxygen-deprived planet, there is one thing about it that gives you a big advantage—light gravity. You can jump seven feet with ease and even clear an eight- or nine-foot-high bar and land as lightly and gracefully as a cat.

Climbing swiftly, you leave the rock monster behind and soon reach the main cavern.

*Turn to page 73.*

You walk briskly away from the bees, then break into a trot. If they come back to the same spot, you'd just as soon not be there. You've only gone about a hundred yards when you come to a crystal-clear spring. What luck! You drink eagerly, fill your canteen, and look around. There's a trail leading off in the other direction; animals must have made the trail, using it as a route to get water. Then you see the most astonishing sight yet—two boys who can't be much older than you tossing a Frisbee! You stand blinking. Is this really the year 3000? Are you really on Venus? The kids stop in their tracks and gape at you. They start to run.

"Hey! Come back!" you yell.

They turn and eye you suspiciously while you approach.

"Where did *you* come from?" one calls.

"That's a long story."

*Turn to page 55*.

It's a long day with only a few rest stops, but you feel lighthearted and happy because the people around you are in such good spirits. Your backpack would weigh forty pounds on Earth, but on Mars it weighs only thirteen. The huge canyon, with its red-pink, and orange-hued rock walls glistening, is the most spectacular sight you've ever seen.

The next time your party stops to rest, you make friends with a boy named Nachim, who is just a year older than you. (Actually he's about a thousand years younger than you, but you can't really count the long period you were in hibernation.)

Nachim tells you that his tribe is the last group of refugees from Earth. "No more can come to the secret colony," he says. "There's too much danger that Styx Mori's commandos will trace us."

*Turn to page 42.*

You run for the river—your only hope is that the giant ants can't swim. Maybe they can't, but it doesn't matter. Big as they are, they run like the wind, and you've made it only halfway to the riverbank when you feel two pincers lifting you as if you were a piece of chicken caught by giant chopsticks. Your last sight is the hideous throat of a giant ant.

**The End**

Later, as your spaceship streaks toward Earth, Osan, the captain, starts to explain his plan.

"Mori ruthlessly seeks out and destroys members of the underground rebel force. Everyone is presumed guilty until proved innocent—"

Suddenly a buzzer sounds. "Battle stations," Osan calls. "A missile, headed toward us!"

You strap yourself into the restraints so you can withstand the high g-forces as the spacecraft maneuvers.

*Whoosh!* The missile streaks by. A cheer goes up.

"Two more . . . three missiles on the way!" The radar man's voice quavers as he speaks.

Osan rests a hand on your shoulder. "There's almost no hope of getting through. We have an escape capsule on board. It's an old Model MW with a Winston computer, the same kind that got you to Mars. It could probably get you to Venus. You have only a few seconds to decide."

*If you eject in the space capsule,
turn to page 74.*

*If you decide to stay with the ship,
turn to page 95.*

You soon learn that the two boys are brothers named Esau and Egon. They lead you back to a village that's no more than a dozen little log houses roofed with strips of the great rubbery leaves taken from the forest floor. You learn that the people there are all descendants of Earth refugees who escaped to Venus almost a hundred years before.

They take you to Norie, the leader of the village. She is a squat, round-faced woman whose age is impossible to guess. The roof of her modest house is propped open to let in the sun and air. Several people sit on either side of you. Egon and Esau sit in a corner

Norie asks you many questions about your experiences. From time to time she looks at the others. Usually they nod, and sometimes they scowl. Norie seems to know what they are thinking. Her face is stern, and you can tell from the expressions of the onlookers they are anxious. But at last she smiles at you.

*Turn to page 141.*

# 56

You rub your bruised head. Gradually you remember what happened. You look outside and breathe a sigh of relief. The capsule, built to withstand a thousand years of space travel, survived the ride through the rapids. What's more, it's nestled right up against the grassy river bank, held from drifting downstream by a fallen tree sticking out from the shore. You can step right out of the capsule and be on your way!

You load your supplies into your backpack and grasp the handle on the hatch door. It turns, but the door won't open. You jiggle the handle, then push against the hatch with all your strength. It still won't budge. It must have jammed when the capsule was being battered in the rapids. You sit there, sweating. You have only a two-week food supply, then the prospect of starvation.

You try to stay calm, to gather your wits. "Winston, the hatch is jammed. Can you open it?"

A moment later your computer replies cheerfully. "I'm sorry. the hatch is designed to be opened manually. I'm not programmed to open it."

*Go on to the next page.*

You rack your brain. You sit helplessly, trying to think.

"Winston," you plead. "Is there nothing we can do?"

Silence; then the answer. "Nothing."

Perhaps because you're more angry than sad, a wild idea comes into your mind. "Winston, fire our rockets and blast off!"

"Sorry. I've thought of that, of course. We aren't positioned properly. Since we're still in the water, we'd just plow a hole in the ground."

*Turn to page 60.*

"Where does everyone live?" you ask.

"That's our house."

Looking up where Nachim is pointing, you see a platform house perched in the upper branches of a flowering tree. A child steps out on the deck and leaps into the air. Swinging on a long dangling vine, she heads your way.

"Here comes my sister, Angela," Nachim says.

*Turn to page 78.*

# 60

Does Winston have a smug tone in his voice, or are you just imagining it? "Winston, what about the retro-rockets?"

"I'm programmed to fire retro-rockets only while we're in flight, and we are not in flight now. Therefore there can be no cause for me to fire them."

*Aha!* Your human brain may yet prove wiser than this computer; after all, it's limited by its programming, sophisticated though it may be.

"Calculate what would happen if we fire the retro-rockets," you demand.

Winston pauses a minute. Finally he speaks. "We would go across to the other side of the river and smash into the rocks on the opposite side."

It's a long shot, but your only shot.

You strap yourself in. "Fire retros!"

*Whoosh. Crash!* The capsule whirls across the river smashing into the rocks, crushing its nose and popping open the hatch! You're shaken up, but not really hurt. And you're free!

*Turn to page 89.*

Gortal makes an entry on his hand-held computer. "You're a special person," he says, "and Styx Mori has decided you should die in a special way. You'll be launched in a new space capsule, equipped with a Winston-class computer just like your old one, only this time it will be programmed to take you directly to the sun."

You try to protest, but your voice is drowned out by Gortal's laughter.

*Turn to page 68.*

You're eager to get back home—no matter what the risks. "I'd like to go on the mission to Earth," you tell Captain Soya.

"I would make the same choice," he says. "We leave tomorrow. You won't have much time for training but you may be very important to us. There are certain things a person your age can accomplish that an older person can't. You're not as likely to arouse suspicion, for one thing."

That afternoon, before you've even had a chance to rest in the small, comfortable room in Captain Soya's house, he calls you to a briefing session and you meet your shipmates: Korro, the pilot, and Nika, a biocomputer expert.

"Here's our plan," Captain Soya begins. "We'll take the sub to Morena, a tiny island that's no more than an extinct volcano rising out of the sea. It's there that our space cruiser is hidden. If Styx Mori's spy satellites are monitoring that part of Venus, they will assume our rocket blast is just a volcanic eruption."

"Won't Mori shoot us down when we approach Earth?" you ask.

*Go on to the next page.*

Captain Soya smiles. "Probably not. Because Styx Mori rules the solar system so completely, he has little fear of attack from space. And his lookout satellites are mostly broken and in disrepair, because his workers won't do anything they aren't forced to do. But to be on the safe side we'll enter Earth's atmosphere on a glide designed to be mistaken for that of an ordinary meteor." Sweeping his hand through the air, he adds, "We'll have to descend at tremendous speed, but we have a triple heat shield to protect us."

You gulp, thinking about the possibility of burning up in the atmosphere.

"We'll attempt to land unnoticed in a remote area in the mountains of Colorado not far from Mori's headquarters," Nika says.

*Turn to page 66.*

You reluctantly hold out your right hand. Styx Mori shakes it with his right hand, slowly increasing the pressure until you cry out with pain.

He presses harder. You scream. You feel your bones breaking! Mori releases your hand and you drop to the floor, writhing in pain.

"Guards!" Mori shouts. "The prisoner is now ready for the firing squad."

## The End

"It's still hard for me to believe Styx Mori took over America," you say.

"He took over *everything.*" Captain Soya places a comforting hand on your shoulder.

"I'll do everything I can to help overthrow this tyrant," you say, "but I don't see what our small group can do. I don't see how we can get close enough to spy on Mori, much less overthrow him."

Captain Soya smiles. His blue eyes glitter as he says, "You'll see, my young friend. Now get to bed early tonight. Our sub leaves for Morena Island at dawn tomorrow. Before the sun sets we'll be cruising in space."

*Turn to page 117.*

It's a beautiful, mild day—a perfect day to set sail! You drag your raft out into the open air and attach the hose from the compressed air canister to the intake valve, then watch with pleasure as the raft slowly inflates. You cut some long strips of cloth from part of the tarpaulin you found and bind them to make ropes. The largest part of the tarpaulin will be your sail, a fallen branch will be your mast, and a paddle will serve as a rudder. Though you can only sail more or less downwind, it doesn't matter, because you don't know which way to go. There is this consolation: No matter which way you go, you will be going south, since you're starting from the north pole!

Equipped with at least a month's supply of nuts, six large canisters of water, and a waterproof cloth in which to catch rain, you push the raft through the gentle surf and set sail.

*Turn to page 70.*

Your capsule is streaking through space. Through the port window you watch the sun grow larger hour by hour.

"*Please* Winston, can't you plot another course?"

"I'm sorry," Winston replies in a soothing tone, "but my circuits aren't working properly. I can tell you that five times nine is forty-five and that four to the third power is sixty-four, if you're interested."

"That won't help us now, Winston. Aren't there some planets we could reach?"

"Sorry," says Winston. "We're heading for the sun and I can't see anything that's not within a thirty-one—degree angle from the sun. My instrument swivels have been disconnected."

You wipe your brow. Though it's still a comfortable temperature in your space capsule, you're sweating just thinking about what's in store for you.

"Please, Winston, aren't there any planets within your field of view?"

"What are planets?" Winston replies.

"Can't you do *anything*?"

Winston hums.

*Go on to the next page.*

You're almost holding your breath, hoping against hope the computer still has some useful functioning capability.

"I can report three objects that are not stars," Winston suddenly announces.

"What are they?"

"A small crescent-shaped object, a large crescent-shaped object, and a disk-shaped object."

"Can you change course to one of them?" you ask.

"I think so," Winston replies. "Which one?"

*If you direct Winston to head for the small crescent, turn to page 80.*

*If you direct him to head for the large crescent, turn to page 84.*

*If you direct him to head for the disk, turn to page 72.*

The wind holds steady, and you're even able to lie back and rest your feet against the mast. Looking around, you see the island getting smaller and smaller. In a way you'll miss it. It was a lonely, desolate place, but it had become your home.

You doze and drift into a deep sleep. When you wake up, you are out of sight of land. You're grateful the wind has held steady. If no storms arise, you feel sure you'll reach shore.

Two days pass. You have no idea how far you've traveled. So far things have gone well, but now the wind is growing stronger and the ocean rougher. Soon whitecaps are everywhere. It's all you can do to hold onto your sail as the little raft pitches and rolls through the choppy sea.

Suddenly a gust of wind rips the mast out of its socket. The sail careens over the side. The raft turns sharply as a wave catches one side of the bow. You try to move toward the high side, but another wave hits. In an instant the raft is upside down, and you're in the water!

At least the water's warm—on Earth at this latitude you wouldn't last more than a few minutes. You're able to turn the raft right-side up, but in vain you look for your backpack. All your supplies have sunk to the bottom. You spot the sail and mast just barely floating about ten feet away.

*If you swim after the sail and mast and try to get them back to the raft, turn to page 91.*

*If you let them sink and concentrate on getting back into the raft, turn to page 109.*

Winston complies with your order. The capsule shifts course, heading for the distant disk-shaped body. Now you can catch up on your sleep. From time to time you wake up. The sun has grown larger. The capsule's cooling system is working almost at full capacity. Well, you think, this must mean you're almost to Venus.

But another day passes; the sun is more off to one side and there's no sign of Venus.

"Winston, are you sure we haven't passed Venus?"

"What's Venus?" replies your damaged computer.

Now you're feeling panicked. Maybe Winston is heading you toward Mercury, the super-hot little planet near the sun, or into the sun itself!

*Turn to page 77.*

As you proceed through the cavern toward the pink-tinted light at the opening, you take a moment to explore along the rock wall. The air smells humid here. You feel the rock with your hand—it's damp!

There's a sort of alcove in the rocks, and at its base is a depression. You rip the lantern off your head and shine it into the space—it's the entrance to an inner cave. You step through and gasp at what you see—a pool, perhaps forty feet across, fed by a trickle of water flowing from the interior wall. Eight thousand feet below the floor of the high desert plateau, water—formed in an ancient age—has been trapped!

You know that the surface of Mars is virtually without water. In the thin dry air the rate of evaporation is tremendous. But down here in this cavern the air pressure is higher than at the surface of the planet, and the cave within the cavern protects the precious cache of water from evaporation.

To say you are excited is an understatement. Water on Mars! You lean over the pond and taste it: fresh and pure as water from a mountain stream!

*Turn to page 79.*

"I'll go," you reply, but even before the words are out of your mouth, Osan shoves you into a metal tube and slams the hatch cover behind you. An air burst catapults you into the space capsule, and a rocket ejects you from the ship. Moments later you observe a red flash against the black backdrop of space. There's no sound, of course, and you can't be sure, but it seems that the ship and its crew have been reduced to space dust.

You're safe for the moment, and your computer, Winston, reports that the capsule is stabilized on course for Venus. Still, you feel more alone and frightened than you've ever been in your life. For a while you just lie there, shivering with anxiety. At last you sleep. If all goes well, your capsule will be close to Venus in the morning.

*Turn to page 13.*

Gortal smiles. "Very well, since you have performed the amazing feat of surviving on both Venus and Mars, Styx Mori will bestow upon you the high honor of shaking your hand."

You have no desire to shake the hand of the most ruthless tyrant in the history of the world, but there is nothing you can do as Gortal marches you down the hall, shoves you into the receiving room and shuts the door behind you.

This time Styx Mori is alone, but you don't have a prayer of overpowering him; you have no weapons, and he is much bigger and stronger than you.

You stand as far away as possible from this odious man, whose cruelty seems etched in the deeply creased lines of his face.

"You are quite amazing to have survived on both Mars and Venus," he says. "Very few could do what you did."

You stand silently, not even acknowledging him with a nod of your head.

"I will let you shake hands with me," he says. "This is a great honor, and other honors for you may follow." There is something far more cruel than friendly in his tone of voice, his leering eyes and his twisted smile, as he steps slowly toward you, his hairy, pudgy hand extended.

*If you shake hands with Styx Mori,
turn to page 64.*

*If you refuse to shake hands, turn to page 130.*

You turn around and start back up the tunnel. The cavern is just ahead of you. You can see light. But as you're about to enter it you notice another narrow tunnel leading off to one side. You poke your head in the opening and hear a muffled grating sound, then silence, then the sound again. Could there be another person wandering through this cavern? you wonder. You feel very lonely and anxious to find some kind of life on this desolate planet.

*If you enter the tunnel to investigate the strange sound, turn to page 37.*

*If you continue on toward the outside of the cavern, turn to page 73.*

The hours pass. You're too exhausted to keep your eyes open. You doze off. When you awake the sun is close and huge and the temperature in the capsule is over a hundred degrees, but the capsule is now on a course at a right angle to the sun. You're already passing the point of closest approach. Gradually, the sun falls behind you, shrinking as you speed away from it.

Winston no longer answers your questions. But looking ahead, you can make out the planet you're headed for—a disk with striped belts on its surface and a red spot near the equator.

Oh no! It's Jupiter—the largest planet, where before you even land you'll be swallowed up in a sea of poisonous gas.

## The End

The young girl swings past and lands on a nearby rock.

"I never thought I'd see this on Mars," you say, grabbing onto a hanging vine.

Suddenly your hair stands on end. Three huge wolflike animals are charging. "Watch out!" you scream.

But Nachim only laughs. "Those are the wehaws. They won't bite—they want us to ride them."

"That looks like fun," you say as you brush the sweat off your brow.

Nachim smiles. "You're going to like it here."

## The End

Where there's water, there may be life! You explore the floor of the cave, looking for clues.

Suddenly a noise coming from the entrance, a hoarse, breathing sound, makes you freeze. Before you can react, a hulking shape, a quadruped—built like a rhino and almost as big—waddles into the cave. The beast is covered with a thick knobby hide. Its eyes are located at the ends of trunks that extend like two flexible horns from its head, the rest of which is nothing but monstrous jaws. It has no nose, but breathes heavily through its jaws, rhythmically exposing a double line of sharp, silvery teeth.

You watch the beast lumber to the water's edge and drink eagerly from the pool, just as you did. There's no doubt in your mind that this creature is a carnivore, and you know you're made of meat! One good thing—it has practically no legs. It must be pretty slow-moving. You're sure you can outrun it.

*If you run for the entrance, turn to page 88.*

*If you stay absolutely still, turn to page 98.*

# 80

"Head for the small crescent," you say.

A rocket fires, diverting the capsule slightly to port, setting it on intersect course with the smaller crescent.

But as you streak through space the sun grows larger still. You can feel its heat even through the full array of shields. The temperature in your tiny cabin rises steadily.

You're thirsty. You know you should conserve water, but you're sweating so much that you have to drink to keep from getting dehydrated. Finally you sleep.

*Turn to page 82.*

Three days later you're on board a space cruiser with six other rebels. Your mission—to capture Styx Mori and deliver him to the rebel leader, known only as Z!

It is a noble thing to try to overthrow a tyrant, but not an easy thing. You learn too late that one of the rebels is in reality a spy for Styx Mori. When your spaceship lands on Earth, Mori's security force is waiting. Within minutes after landing, your spaceship is flooded with sleeping gas. You struggle vainly to stay awake. . . .

*Turn to page 23.*

When you awake the heat is unbearable. The sun looks huge. Looking out the rear window, you see a brilliant planet. It has no moon—it must be Venus!

"Winston, we must have passed Venus! Can't we turn back?"

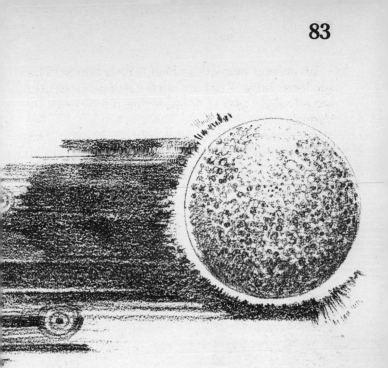

"The square root of six hundred twenty-five is twenty-five," Winston replies.

Suddenly you realize what's happened: Your space capsule is headed for Mercury, the planet closest to the sun—so close that its surface temperature is well over a thousand degrees. You might as well be locked on your original course to the sun itself.

**The End**

An aiming rocket fires almost the moment you give the command. Though Winston can no longer name the planets, you're convinced the large crescent must be Venus. What a relief that Winston's navigational and propulsion systems are still working!

During the next hours you get as much sleep as you can; you know you're going to need it once you land.

*Turn to page 13*.

You refuse to give up hope. Somehow you'll make it through! You eat fewer nuts each day so that your supply will last longer. You build a wall of loose rocks against your pile of leaves so that they stack up higher. That way you're able to sleep under more leaves and keep snug and warm even when the temperature drops below freezing.

One day you notice a glow on the horizon. The sky is getting brighter. The next day it's brighter still. You can see the outlines of trees and rocks again. How can spring be coming so soon? It seems like a miracle. Then you remember what you once learned during a visit to the planetarium: Because Venus is closer to the sun than the Earth is, it travels faster and has a shorter distance to travel each circuit around the sun. Venus's year is a good deal shorter than an Earth year, and so winter is shorter too! Spring—and the sun—will soon arrive!

Within a week there is enough light for you to gather more nuts. Now you know you're going to make it! When the sun rises again, you'll set out in your raft; you'll get to the mainland and find Earth people, and then . . . Well, that's too far ahead to think about. Right now you're happy—for the first time in a long time.

*Turn to page 67.*

As you reveal that ninety-seven people are living in Caverna, a cruel smile breaks out across Gruford's face.

"Ninety-seven to eliminate," he says, rubbing his hands gleefully. "Styx Mori will be glad to hear of our work."

"Leader," one of the guards speaks up. "We'll each receive gold medals with the seal of Styx Mori set in fine rubies. Think of it—a chance to kill ninety-seven rebels!"

Grufurd smiles at the guard. Then, pointing at you, he says, "Ninety-eight!"

**The End**

You run for the entrance of the cave, watching the creature out of the corner of your eye. It looks up at you but doesn't move, and you take a moment to look back, feeling more curious now than frightened. The beast waves its eye trunks as if trying to see you from different angles. Then, jaws open, it starts toward you. You turn and run—into the teeth of the creature's mate! She had only been coming to drink, but instead enjoys a delicious meal.

**The End**

You climb out of your ruptured capsule. It feels great to stand on solid ground. Though you've landed far north of the tropics, the temperature must be ninety degrees even in the shade of these huge broad-leafed trees. The ground cover consists of huge dead leaves piled on each other like sheets of greenish-brown rubber. They form a thick carpet that seems to prevent other plants from growing except for occasional giant ferns.

You wander a ways into the forest looking for signs of edible plants or animals or some sign of human life. There are many kinds of birds in this forest. You can't see them, but you can hear their beautiful songs; the songs sound like the trilling of oboes and flutes. Sometimes you spot a flash of bright color in the leaf canopy high above or behind a giant fern. Insects seem absent, and you're glad about that even though you suspect that there are hordes of them in the layers of fallen leaves beneath your feet.

Suddenly you hear a rumbling in the forest floor. Some heavy animals must be stalking through the forest. Then you see them. A great troop of beasts that look like giant ants, supergiant ants, almost as big as elephants! And they will be passing you on both sides!

---

*If you run for the river, turn to page 52.*

*If you stay absolutely motionless, turn to page 96.*

You hurl the rock and hit the hulk between the eyes. It topples backward, bellowing, onto the other hulk. The little seal flops safely into the water. Other seals are watching. Two of them swim toward you, barking as if to thank you. Another places its flippers over the edge of the pool; it seems to want to touch you. You'd like to play with the seals, but now both hulks are lumbering around the edge of the pool, and there's no doubt they're headed for you! You race for the entrance; you're about three steps away when you stop in your tracks: Another hulk is coming into the cave!

There's a rock near your feet. Maybe you can knock the beast out of the way. But one of the two hulks chasing you is so close, it may get you before you can throw the rock. In the split second of time you consider the only other option—to dive into the pool!

*If you grab the rock and fight the hulks, turn to page 146.*

*If you dive into the pool, turn to page 100.*

You swim as fast as you can, desperate to grab the mast and the sail before they sink. In a minute you have a firm grip on them. Now you start stroking for the raft with one arm, holding on to the mast with the other, but the wind is blowing the raft away from you. You take one more stroke before realizing how fast the raft is drifting downwind. Panicked, you let go of the mast and sail and swim all out for the raft. In a few seconds you realize the awful truth—the raft is drifting faster than you can swim. Your life can last only as long as you can tread water.

**The End**

Suruma, a frail, elderly man, receives you at his house—the largest in Caverna. It's set on a high bluff overlooking the lake. He listens attentively to your story, but when you ask for his permission to journey to the surface, he silences you with a sweeping motion of his hand.

"We are safe here in Caverna only because the Earth tyrant does not know that we exist. Styx Mori thinks Mars is a desolate, almost uninhabitable planet. That, my young friend, is the only reason he leaves us alone. If I were to let you go up to the surface, you might meet up with his commandos or even find your way back to Earth. Then he would find out that there is another little village left to conquer."

"But I would keep it secret," you insist.

Suruma shakes his head. "I want to trust you, my young friend, but Styx Mori has ways of making people talk—ways you would not even want to hear about. I'm sorry, but you must stay here for the rest of your life. To make sure that neither you nor anyone else ever escapes, I shall seal the only entrance to Caverna at once."

*Turn to page 135.*

Within moments after eating the wax from a hive of killer bees, you begin to feel the strangest sensations. You feel as if your body is shrinking; your arms flattening and thinning; legs growing, front and back; your eyes bulging . . . bulging. You begin to hum, a hum that turns into a high-pitched, droning sound. Your whole body seems to be vibrating.

You haven't turned into a bee; but you think you have!

**The End**

"I'll stay," you say at once.

Osan squeezes your shoulder affectionately. "You're a brave one," he says.

"More missiles!" the radar operator reports.

"Evasive program!" Osan commamds.

The computer acknowledges Osan's command. But the ship remains on course.

"Evasive program futile," the computer says calmly. "All courses and speeds on intersect."

Osan rubs his forehead with his fingers. You can't see his eyes. He doesn't want you to see his face. He doesn't want to tell you, but you know anyway—there's no hope of survival. Styx Mori has won again.

## The End

You freeze; you don't dare to breathe. The giant ants, their heads bobbing above you, lumber past. None of them looks at you. It's as if you weren't even there. You stand very still, shaking, wondering why you're still alive. If they had been elephants, they would never have missed you. Maybe these creatures are "hard-wired"—genetically programmed to respond only to something that moves. You've heard that frogs will starve to death before they snap at a fly that's not moving. In their minds if it's not moving, it's not food. But why are you daydreaming? You've got to figure out how to survive on this weird planet!

You look around for some clue as to which way to go. But your attention is quickly diverted by a buzzing noise. A bee is flying by. Except for its unusual crimson color you might mistake it for a common bumblebee on Earth.

ZZZZZZZ . . . ZZZZ . . . ZZZZZZZ. . . . You wish it wouldn't buzz near you like that. . . . Here it comes again! ZZZZZZZZ. . . . It soars away.

Maybe it thinks you're a Venutian flower. You're almost sorry to see it go. It made you feel a little less lonely.

But now the bee is returning—with others! They're surrounding you! ZZZZZ ZZZZZZZZ. . . . They haven't attacked yet. Maybe they won't. Maybe they will. In the distance you see still more bees flying toward you. What is this? You've never seen bees act this way before.

*Go on to the next page.*

You feel like running, but it seems certain they'd follow. Anyway, it's too late. A huge swarm is circling your head, buzzing in a variety of pitches that sound like one harmonic chord.

Now they swoop off in the direction of the sun. Then they circle back, then spiral off again, their movements perfectly coordinated. It's almost as if they want you to come with them!

*If you go the other way, turn to page 50.*

*If you follow the bees, turn to page 103.*

You stand motionless, hoping the hulking creature won't see you. The beast drinks, then waves its eye trunks. They train directly at you. It bends over and drinks again. Apparently it didn't classify you as a possible source of food.

It looks up again, this time pointing its eyes toward the entrance. Another of the hulks has arrived. The second one waddles over to the pond and begins to drink. Then you watch in amazement as they lumber over to a far wall and tuck in their heads and eye trunks so as to look like a couple of large boulders.

*Turn to page 107.*

Working by the meager light of the stars, you inflate your raft and load it with supplies. Your plan is to prop up the tarpaulin for a sail and hope the wind will take you to a safe shore.

Finally your raft is ready. You launch it into the surf, but in the near-darkness you can't see the big wave coming. In a second your raft is over, spilling you into the cold water. You clutch frantically for your supply of green nuts, but it's too dark to see. You know they are lost, and that you are too.

**The End**

Your situation seems hopeless, but you don't have time to think about that. You sidestep the oncoming hulk and, with a twisting motion, arms outstretched, dive into the pool. In an instant you're surrounded by the friendly seals. The hulks hover at the edge, snapping their huge jaws, but they dare not enter. In their own element the seals are masters. But that does you little good—you can't tread water forever. And the hulks show no sign of leaving.

One of the seals tugs at your clothes, then starts to dive and pull you along. Another does the same. Are they trying to drown you? They seemed so friendly and intelligent!

Then you understand. They want you to dive. But how could they help you that way? Maybe they don't understand that you can't breathe underwater. Then something occurs to you. These seals—so much like ones on Earth—don't breathe underwater either. They came from somewhere that's open to the air.

There's nothing to lose. You take a deep breath and dive. The seals dive with you, nudging you along. They are guiding you through an underwater tunnel. But you have no idea how long the tunnel is, and your breath is soon running out. You can't last much longer!

*If you turn back, turn to page 147.*

*If you swim on, turn to page 104.*

Gortal looks you up and down before speaking. "Styx Mori likes you so much, he has decided not to kill you right away. Instead, he will let you freeze to death on Mars."

You try to protest, but it's no use. Styx Mori has no understanding of mercy and compassion. A few days later you are launched again in a standard space capsule. Its computer—the familiar "Winston" model—is programmed to take you to Mars.

It's a three-day flight before your space capsule settles into Martian orbit. You feel so depressed and sad, you can hardly think, but after three or four passes around the red planet, you realize you'll just starve if you stay out in space. You ask Winston if he can find a good place to land.

"Certainly," Winston replies. "I've obeyed the Supreme Emperor's program. Now I'm free to help you."

*Turn to page 14.*

You follow the mysterious magnetic bees through the exotic forest, tramping on the rubbery leaves.

At last you come to a great grove of stately trees, their massive exposed roots spread out like buttresses of a cathedral. The air is filled with the harmonic drone of bees. As you stand there, filled with awe at the beauty of your surroundings and the strange feeling it gives you to be inside a city of bees, thoughts flow into your mind. Somehow you know they are coming from the bees. You suddenly understand that when the bees come together in large enough numbers, they gain a collective intelligence—a wisdom found only rarely among humans.

From the bees you learn that they do not seek power over humans or any other creatures. Their only desire is to be left alone.

Now you sense that they are listening to *your* thoughts—even to thoughts that you're not thinking now, but that lie within your mind, thoughts you might think sometime, perhaps tonight as you are going to sleep. Now the bees are telling you about a path through the forest, a path they know you should follow.

*Turn to page 120.*

Though your lungs are straining to the utmost, you swim as smoothly and swiftly as you can, following the seals through the tunnel. Why is it so long? you wonder. You wish you could turn back, but you can't now, you'd never make it.

You fight the urge to breathe underwater. Your lungs are bursting. Then the tunnel ends abruptly, and you shoot up to the surface, gasping for air. You're almost too exhausted to swim, but the friendly seals buoy you up; all you have to do is relax as they nudge you steadily toward shore. In a few moments your feet touch bottom. You pat and stroke the nearest seals by way of thanking them, and gratefully step out onto a smooth sandy beach.

Looking around, you see that you surfaced in a lake that's at least a mile long. The lake and its surroundings are in a vast cavern. It takes you a moment to see where the light is coming from. High on the walls of the canyon, perhaps a hundred feet or more above the ground, are evenly spaced lamps, each of which looks like a full moon on Earth. By this light you can see the rolling floor of the cavern. Little cottages and long low buildings are scattered about. One might mistake this scene for some part of the Sahara, for there are no trees, nor even grass.

*Go on to the next page.*

You've found intelligent life on Mars! No doubt of that. But who lives here? Are they refugees from Earth, persons who fled here to escape the tyranny of Styx Mori? Or are they Martians, who, finding their planet drying up, their atmosphere becoming as thin as the air that blows across the highest mountaintops of Earth, were forced to build a civilization far underground where sufficient water and oxygen remained?

*Turn to page 116.*

Slowly you work your way toward the entrance. Before you've taken more than a few cautious steps, the water surface breaks. Two, then three, four . . . almost a dozen small seallike creatures press their flippers against the side of the pool. They peer anxiously around, then one by one scramble across the floor of the cave to a wall between you and the hulks. Rearing up on their hind flippers, they gnaw at the stalactites that have formed on the roof of the cave. What a curious food, you think, especially for an animal that looks as if it should be eating fish! Suddenly the hulks uncoil, their eye trunks fixed on the seals, their jaws opening wide as they lumber clumsily toward the feeding animals. Instantly the seals begin scrambling back into the water. They aren't fast but neither are the hulks. It looks as if the seals will make it, except for one little seal that seems to have a lame flipper. It isn't going to make it back to the pool.

There's a rock nearby. You have a strong urge to hurl it at the hulk closest to the baby seal.

*If you throw the rock, turn to page 90.*

*If you decide not to interfere, turn to page 124.*

# 108

You want to do what you can to help overthrow Styx Mori, but you're not willing to risk insanity.

When he hears your refusal, Dr. Haass nods. "I don't blame you. Look, you'll be leaving for Earth soon. Take this vial. Always keep it in your pocket. It's waterproof. Someday you may need it."

You look at the black plastic capsule about the size of a robin's egg.

"When will I need it?" you ask.

"When the time comes you will know."

"What should I do when I need it?"

Dr. Haass looks at you with a cold steady gaze. "Break it."

You thrust the capsule in your pocket. It's time to meet your space crew.

*Turn to page 81.*

It takes all your strength, but you manage to flip the raft over and climb back in. The mast and sail have already sunk out of sight. You sit shivering in a puddle of cold water with no food, no sails, and no paddles. Your backpack is gone, and you're lost on an ocean of unknown size on a strange planet a thousand years in the future. It's hard to imagine a more hopeless situation. Then you see what looks like a pipe sticking out of the water. It's moving slowly toward you. It looks like a periscope! You wave frantically, but the periscope, or whatever it is, turns away and drops below the surface.

*Turn to page 126.*

Boldly you step forward, and suddenly you are inside the sphere, floating in a space that seems to contain nothing but glowing, misty patches of light. And looking at your body, you see that it, too, is glowing softly—a smoky bluish apparition. You feel as if you no longer exist. You feel you are no longer in the present.

All light dims. All goes black. All is silent. Though you're still conscious, you haven't the slightest sensation, nor even awareness of your body, until . . . you *are* aware—and aware you're in your own time and on Earth and reading this book!

Dr. Grambling was right! A time machine would be invented by the year 3000, and you were lucky enough to find it!

**The End**

"It's kind of scary," you say. "Supersmart killer bees."

"Fortunately," Dr. Haass continues, "they aren't hostile to us so far. They realize that we are peaceful, friendly people and mean them no harm. In fact, they are our allies because they are aware that Styx Mori would like to wipe them out. In fact, they may be our only hope of overthrowing the tyrant of Earth! Apparently he's afraid of no man or beast, except for these little bees. Because of them he is afraid to set foot on this beautiful planet."

"Is there any way we can communicate with them?"

Dr. Haass leans close to you. "If you eat some wax from a hive, certain enzymes will change your brain structure and you may be able to communicate with them. But I must warn you: There is a risk in trying this. It's possible that you will lose your very sanity. Are you willing to take that chance?"

*If you say yes, turn to page 94.*

*If you refuse, turn to page 108.*

When Captain Soya returns sometime later, he peers through the periscope and then motions for you to look. The submarine has entered a large grotto. The roof and sides of the cavern appear to be made of deeply pitted volcanic rock that reflects shades of pink and ochre in the light of the lanterns hanging from the walls. The water is the most delicate shade of blue. Ahead is a dock where two other midget submarines are tied up. Beyond them is a group of small buildings.

"Where are we?" you ask as the sub gently rises to the surface.

Soya looks at you intently. "We are at the secret base of the United Democracies of Earth."

You smile, thinking for a moment he might be joking, but his expression shows no trace of irony.

"All freedom has been extinguished on Earth, you see. Only a few hundred Earth people are free today and none of them are living on their own planet. They are hiding out in tiny little bands scattered about on Mars and Venus."

*Turn to page 150.*

You soon find yourself locked in a cell. A talkative guard tells you that Styx Mori has sent commandos to seek out and destroy any refugees from Earth. Although Mori has decided Mars isn't worth colonizing, he can't bear the thought that anyone may be living in freedom on the red planet. His solution is simple: Find every person living there and kill them.

The guard stops talking as Grufurd, the bearded leader of the commandos, enters. He looks at you contemptuously. There is no compassion, no humanity, nor even curiosity in his steel-gray eyes. You're certain you're about to receive the death sentence.

Grufurd flips a gleaming eight-inch long stiletto from hand to hand as he speaks. "We know there are more refugees on this planet, but we haven't been able to find them. We have food and oxygen supplies for only six more days; then we must return to Earth."

The blade leaps from the stiletto. He slowly swings it until it's pointed at your throat.

"Tell us where there are more refugees, and I will take you back to Earth and see that you are comfortable there. Otherwise you will be taken out, and my men will cut you up into little pieces."

---

*If you say that you have not seen anyone since you landed in the space capsule, turn to page 43.*

*If you tell Grufurd about the community living in Caverna, turn to page 86.*

# 114

The next day Captain Soya leads you through an underground tunnel that winds through the porous volcanic substratum. After a half-day journey you reach the surface again, exiting from an opening at the base of a cliff. You find yourself in a majestic forest. Each of the gigantic, widely spaced trees rises three hundred feet before branching out into a canopy of enormous fan-shaped leaves. The air is bathed in soft green light, the effect of the sun shining through the forest canopy. The scene is beautiful and peaceful—except for bees buzzing about. You wonder if they are the killer bees that the captain said hadn't killed anyone yet. Presently you reach a large clearing, which is the setting for a number of modest log houses.

*Turn to page 122.*

"Who are *you*?" A man's voice interrupts your thoughts.

You whirl and confront a short, solidly built man, dressed in crudely fashioned blue pants and shirt. His thick hair and beard form a gray wreath around his ruddy, weathered face.

"Where did you come from?" he asks before you can answer.

"It's quite a long story."

"Well, come with me then," he says in a polite though guarded tone. "There are many here in Caverna who will want to talk to you." Offering you his hand, he says, "My name is Tibor, by the way."

*Turn to page 118.*

You're en route to Earth on the rebel ship *Osprey*. As your ship approaches Earth, sensors report that Styx Mori's radar scanners are on full array. The meaning of this is clear. Mori has learned of the rebel activity in space.

"We can't approach Earth's stratosphere," Captain Soya tells you. "We're going to turn back. But you can still get to Earth's surface by using the Mark Nine Hundred space capsule."

"Okay, if that's the way it is." You'll go to Earth alone.

*Turn to page 123.*

Tibor leads you to his simple stone cottage, where you meet his wife, Tan, and his brother, Andras. You learn they are indeed descendants of refugees from Earth who discovered this great cavern and settled here hundreds of years ago. A small fusion reactor powers the lamps that line the cavern walls and provide its only light. The ninety-seven people who live here survive by growing vegetables hydroponically in tanks. Their only other food are fish from the lake and edible crystals found in the stalactites. The government of Caverna is tribal. The chief, called Suruma, is the sole ruler, though even he is bound by law and custom.

"I guess Suruma will want to meet me." you say.

"Indeed, he will," Tibor replies, "but if he does, he will see to it that you don't leave Caverna for the rest of your life. He is afraid that if anyone leaves he or she will reveal our secret location to the Earth tyrant, Styx Mori. We don't mind staying here—it is our home—but for you it may seem like a prison."

*Go on to the next page.*

"How can I reach the surface of Mars?" you ask.

"We can't show you the way," Tibor says. "If we were caught helping you escape, we would be imprisoned. But I will tell you how to find it. It is a difficult journey. If you safely reach the surface, you may be able to team up with some other Earth people who have a settlement on the surface not far from where you exit. But I must warn you—it's easier to stay alive in Antarctica than on the surface of Mars."

*If you decide to meet the chief, Suruma, turn to page 93.*

*If you decide to try to escape to the surface, turn to page 125.*

Following the bees' directions, you travel along a twisting path that winds higher and higher until you reach a plateau covered only with grass and clumps of gnarled, copper-colored shrubs. You gasp at what you see before you—a perfect silver sphere, about six feet in diameter, hovering silently only a few inches above the grass as if suspended by some magical force.

You walk cautiously up to the sphere. There are no doors or windows. It is a thing of pure beauty, and you feel no reason to fear it. You try to touch it, and your hand passes through its surface as if there were nothing there. You press your other hand forward, and it, too, passes freely through the surface of the sphere. Is the sphere real, you wonder, or is it only a hologram?

*Turn to page 110.*

"This is Amozia," says Captain Soya. "And here comes Dr. Haass!"

A tiny man—he can't be more than four feet high—strides briskly toward you. You're not sure he's even human. His hair looks like fur, his neck is astonishingly long, and his arms look almost like steel cables.

"Venus is a world of mutations," Dr. Soya whispers. "Dr. Haass is a member of a new species of hominids. He may look strange to you, but remember that you look strange to him too."

You thank Captain Soya for his kindness and join Dr. Haass for a tour of the beehives hanging from some of the trees. "These are called killer bees," he says, "because their sting is lethal. But they do not sting unless they are very angry or unless their lives are threatened. That much is not very remarkable. But what is remarkable is the intelligence of these bees. No single one of them is more intelligent than an ordinary bee, yet they have a means of communicating with each other by exchanging almost imperceptible electromagnetic pulses, similar to exchanges between nerve cells in the human brain. As a result, when enough bees are in the same area, they develop a *collective* intelligence. Once a bee has been in a swarm, it gains some part of the collective wisdom. To tell the truth, we still don't understand how the process works."

*Turn to page 111.*

Your perilous entry through your home planet's atmosphere goes well. The Mark 900 is designed to give the trajectory and infrared signature of a common meteorite. If it showed up on Mori's radar screens, it was ignored by the master computer, because your capsule lands smoothly and safely near the edge of a deserted pasture somewhere in Colorado. You quickly camouflage it with sticks and brush and set out to find a house or a farm, hoping you'll stumble on someone who will befriend you.

At the far end of the pasture you come to a road. An air van is approaching. You wonder whether you should flag it down or keep out of sight. But there's no time to think. The van swerves toward you, braking noiselessly. Three uniformed men jump out—laser guns drawn.

One of them throws a net over you. The others pull each end of a rope, and instantly you are trussed from head to toe. Moments later you find yourself in the van with dozens of other captives. It lifts off and skims across the countryside.

Bruised and aching, you murmur to the captive beside you, "Where are they taking us?"

"To a work camp," a man replies bitterly. "This is the way Styx Mori recruits volunteers."

*Turn to page 162.*

The other seals hang on at the edge of the pool, frantically barking and squealing as the hulks finish their meal. Then the seals dive and disappear from sight. You start toward the cave entrance, but without your having noticed, a third hulk has arrived, blocking your escape! Suddenly they are all charging, their huge jaws snapping.

You have no choice. You run three steps and dive into the pool, splashing water on the oncoming hulks. Thankfully they stop short at the edge. For the moment you are safe. But that doesn't bother the hulks. They quietly sit in a circle around the pool. You can tell they are prepared to wait— for longer than you can swim. You'll keep paddling as long as you can. You'd rather drown than be eaten.

## The End

You suspect it would be easier to escape to Mars's surface after dark. Tibor confirms this.

"We have no TV here in Caverna," he says. "People usually read or play games or work at their hobbies for a few hours and then go to bed."

"I won't run into anyone then?"

"I hope not, though the way may be guarded. Once you reach the surface, you must climb to the top of the mesa. From there the way will be clear."

Just as daytime is artificial in Caverna, so is the night. After dinner the lamps on the cavern walls are gradually dimmed so as to produce about the same amount of light you would have on Earth on a moonlit night.

A few minutes later you bid Tibor and his family good-bye and set out along a steep and rocky path that leads along one side of the cavern wall.

Though you must travel only three or four miles to reach the tunnel leading to the surface, you have to feel your way along. In the dim light there's always the danger of stumbling. A turned ankle would end your bid for freedom. But you doggedly keep on, step after step, reaching the tunnel entrance just as the cavern lights are turned up for the next day. Before starting the long, steep climb to the surface, you rest in the shelter of some rocks and eat some of the crystal food you stuffed in your pack before leaving.

*Turn to page 129.*

A few minutes later, like a whale surfacing, a miniature submarine rises out of the water! Two men appear on deck as the sub pulls alongside, and they pull you aboard.

"Quick, get below!" one man says nervously.

The other man secures the hatch behind you. Within seconds the sub is diving.

Captain Soya, a short bearded man, shakes his head as you huddle under a blanket sipping hot tea and telling the story of your wanderings.

"You're the strangest thing I've seen on Venus," he says. "We almost didn't pick you up—we thought you might be a spy for Styx Mori, the tyrant of Earth."

"And a submarine is the last thing I expected to see on Venus," you reply.

"We've picked up the diaphone signal, Captain," a crew member says.

"Take her in," the skipper replies.

"Where are we headed?" you inquire.

"Be patient and you'll see. I have work to do."

*Turn to page 112.*

# 128

After deciding to stay on the island, you content yourself with fixing up your dugout and decorating it with driftwood and crab shells and pebbles to make it seem more like a home. Each day the sun sinks lower in the sky until one day it does not rise at all. The temperature drops to around sixty degrees, the wind blows, and for the first time on Venus, you actually feel cold.

You gather nuts and store them in your bunker. The days are growing darker. Soon it will be pitch-dark all day long, just the way it is in winter at the earth's North Pole. You gather leaves and pile them in one corner of your bunk; they will serve as your bed and blanket during the dark winter months ahead. You wonder how cold winter will get, how long it will last, and whether you will survive it.

*Turn to page 134.*

Now you are in the steep winding tunnel. Except for places along the way where phosphorus embedded in the rock gives off an eerie green light, you have to move in total darkness. You feel exhausted and discouraged. From time to time you think of turning back. But just as you are about to give up hope, you see light up ahead. The tunnel bends, and suddenly the entrance is only a few feet away!

You start to run, but stop short, gasping for air; the air up here is extremely thin, you notice. You take a deep breath from your oxygen bottle. Cautiously you peer out at the Martian desert.

*Turn to page 137.*

# 130

Vowing never to shake hands with this tyrant, you thrust your hands deep into your pockets. You feel the egg-shaped capsule Dr. Haass gave you on Venus.

"You *dare* to refuse my handshake!" Styx Mori is red with anger. He levels a laser gun at your head. You dig your thumbnail into the capsule in your pocket. You can feel the shell crack. In a second you feel something crawling up the palm of your hand. You gently curl your fingers partway around it and pull your hand out of your pocket.

"Prepare to die," Styx Mori says.

But at that moment you open your hand, holding your palm toward Styx Mori so he can see the Venutian bee perched on your palm.

A scream escapes from the tyrant's lips. In an instant the guards are at the door. The bee is suddenly in the air, hovering above Mori's head.

"Send the guards away or die!" you shout.

*"Out! Out!"* Mori screams.

The guards retreat.

"Your laser gun, Mori."

The bee zooms in tight circles above the tyrant's head.

"Please, please." He cowers before you begging you to take his laser gun.

*Go on to the next page.*

You grab it and step back. "Now, remember, one wrong move and you die. Pick up your telephone. Order your forces to surrender to Z."

"No, please!" Mori pleads.

"NOW!"

As if stirred by your voice, the bee dives toward Mori's eyes. He covers his face with one arm, cringing. You hand him his radiophone.

"NOW!"

*Turn to page 143.*

Early the next morning you join a group of people trekking across the Martian desert toward the space station. Everyone wears a poncho, camouflaged to blend with the red desert landscape. Though the air is very thin, the wind blows so hard it almost knocks you off your feet. The sun is high overhead; it's too far away to warm you much. You shiver as you plod along the trail, step by weary step.

Tokan, the leader, is always looking up toward the red-tinted sky. He's watching for Styx Mori's commandos. If their scouter craft comes near, everyone must instantly drop to the ground and hide under his or her poncho.

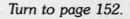

*Turn to page 152.*

# 134

For the next month you live in total darkness, a darkness that at times you feel will drive you mad. There is not even a moon to comfort you—Venus has none. At least there are the stars, the same wonderful array of constellations you saw from Earth a thousand years before. The Milky Way, stretching across the sky, looks like a trail of glowing grains of sand. One "star," far brighter than any of the others, is a beautiful mix of green, blue, and white. You know it is not a star at all, but your own planet, Earth. And more than anything else it is the sight of Earth that gives you hope and courage to make it through the dark, lonely, endless night.

*Turn to page 139.*

Suruma arranges for you to live with Tibor and his family. You love working by the lake and helping to train the seals to bring fish to shore, and soon you know many of these intelligent and friendly animals by name. You consider them, along with many people in Caverna, to be your good friends.

Life is not bad, and there's plenty of time for play, but you miss the sun, the trees, and the grass, and you miss Earth. Someday, you vow, you'll find a way to return home.

**The End**

Everywhere you look is the red, rock-strewn plain. There's no sign of life, no plants, no clouds in the sky; only the sun, both smaller and less brilliant than on Earth. At least you can feel its heat. The temperature here must be almost fifty degrees. This is what it's like at midday in the Martian tropics. But night will be a far different story. When the sun sets, the temperature will drop by a hundred degrees. You know you must find the settlement Tibor mentioned before nightfall, or you'll be frozen solid by morning.

A few hundred yards to the north is the mesa Tibor mentioned. You make your way slowly toward it, trying to use as little oxygen as possible.

*Go on to the next page.*

It takes you a full hour to reach the top of the mesa, but you're rewarded with the sight you've wanted so much to see—the plastic dome of the Earth settlers, which is camouflaged with red-and-brown patterns. You run toward it, jumping across the small rocks and darting around the big ones. In the light gravity of Mars you can run like a deer. There will be plenty of oxygen at the space dome, so you gulp greedily from your own supply.

As you head toward the entrance two men run out; they are wearing military uniforms and each of them holds a laser pistol aimed right at you. On their arm sleeves is an insignia, an X in a circle. They don't look like the rebels you expected to find. In a moment you realize that you've walked right into the hands of commandos in service to the tyrant Styx Mori.

*Turn to page 113.*

Six weeks have passed. You're still alive. Though it's winter at the north pole, the temperature is still above freezing most of the time. Winter at the north pole here is no colder than winter along the coast of Georgia. Still, you often shiver, lying in your dugout, huddled under a pile of leaves. In the dark you count the remaining nuts in your supply. There are only enough to last a few weeks more; yet darkness at the North Pole on Earth lasts almost six months, doesn't it? You've been living in darkness for almost three months now, and you've never felt so depressed in your life.

*If you rig up your raft and set out in darkness, turn to page 99.*

*If you decide to wait it out, turn to page 85.*

In a few minutes you round the bend in the canyon wall. Your heart leaps for joy. A stream of water is spouting out of the side of a cliff and falling into a little pond. Near the edge of the pond is a small building made of red Martian rocks. Rows of windows look out over the canyon floor. A radar antenna is mounted on the roof, and alongside the pond is a greenhouse. You can see plants inside! As you run toward the building a man walks out of the greenhouse, yelling. You shrink back, but he calls, "Don't be afraid."

You notice a young girl peering through a window. A woman comes toward you from the main building. In a few minutes you're surrounded by a dozen friendly, curious humans!

You soon learn you've found friends—Earth people who are refugees from the tyrant Styx Mori! After hearing the story of your adventures, they welcome you as a member of the rebel forces. Their goal is to one day overthrow the tyrant of Earth and reestablish true democracy as the form of government there. They tell you that you are at a halfway station between the rebels' space station and a secret colony. If you join the group headed for the space station, you will be expected to go on a dangerous mission to Earth on behalf of the rebels. Caravans leave for both places in the morning.

---

*If you decide to go on the caravan headed for the secret colony, turn to page 39.*

*If you decide to go on the caravan headed for the space station, turn to page 132.*

"We are satisfied you are telling the truth," Norie says, "and you are not a spy of Styx Mori's. We welcome you as a member of our community. You may live in the house of your new friends, Esau and Egon."

A cheer goes up, and everyone in the room hugs you—even the leader herself.

*Turn to page 157.*

Whimpering, the tyrant of Earth clears his throat, then slowly picks up the phone. "Code CQE Three. Order of the Emperor," he says in the dull, mechanical voice of a broken man. "Surrender immediately to Z."

Mori gently lays down the phone. "It's in my hair!" he screams.

"Don't make a move," you say calmly, "or it will drive its stinger into your scalp."

Mori hangs his head, eyes tightly closed, shivering with fear. A half hour later, the door opens. A frail elderly woman with flowing white hair enters the room. She taps the floor with her cane as she walks toward you. Behind her are six guards in rebel uniforms.

"I am Z," she says.

"You?"

She nods. "I've been waiting a long time for this moment." Taking your hand she says, "I am very grateful to you. Today the people of Earth are free again. May it always be so."

**The End**

# 144

Cautiously you turn the latch handles on the escape hatch and open the door a crack. Instantly it blows open, sweeping you outside in a rush of air. Your ears pop. You gasp for breath. You find yourself sitting on the hard rusty-colored sand. You're afraid you're going to suffocate in the thin Martian air, but soon you feel better. There's enough air here to breathe. Winston knew what he was doing; you're in an oxygen-rich pocket far below the average elevation of the Martian surface. If you can survive a few days, your body will become used to the thin air, as is the case on Earth with travelers to high altitudes.

You look around the dry, lifeless landscape. There's not a tree or cactus or bit of sagebrush in sight. No birds, not even an ant or a fly. But your heart leaps as you notice an opening in the side of the canyon wall. The top of the opening is an almost perfect arch, surely carved by intelligent creatures, perhaps by the human refugees from Earth that Winston told you about! You return to the capsule and take the lantern from your survival kit. Though you're still having some trouble breathing, you feel light as a bird—you weigh about a third of what you would on Earth.

*Go on to the next page.*

With your lantern strapped onto your head like
a coal miner's lamp, you step through the opening,
which leads to an area about the size of a large
room. Along one wall you find a narrow tunnel.
You'd like to see where it leads, but it tips down so
steeply, you're afraid that you'll lose your footing
and slip.

*If you take a chance on going down into the
tunnel, turn to page 25.*

*If you decide to go back outside and explore
along the canyon floor, turn to page 44.*

You grab the rock and hurl it into the open jaws of the hulk coming at you from the entrance. It reels backward, but before you can get past, it grabs your leg in its jaws. You scream with pain as you try to twist free. A second later another hulk is upon you, and then another, and another. . . .

**The End**

It's too risky. You're really scared. You twist around and streak back for the surface. The seals turn with you and nudge you so you can break water as soon as possible. You feel exhausted, and the hulks are still there. You want to dive again, but now you're too tired to try. You look up at the hulks sitting by the pool, their eye trunks trained on you. You paddle toward the middle of the pond, as far away from them as possible. You have enough strength to keep treading water . . . for a while.

**The End**

You run into the cavern, but the floor drops off sharply. Suddenly you're sliding, down, down the steep slope—into a nest of rock monsters.

**The End**

After the sub has surfaced Captain Soya invites you to join him on the deck while the others steer the little vessel into the dock. Some people on shore run up to help cleat the docking lines.

"Thanks to the perfection of fusion power in the twenty-third century," Soya continues, "energy is now easily generated. And Venus is rich in natural food sources, but the climate is so strange, and there are so many dangerous creatures—killer bees, for instance—that Styx Mori has chosen not to colonize the planet."

"Killer bees! I hope there aren't any here!" you say.

"There are indeed," the captain replies. "But they have extraordinary intelligence, and they don't kill us, at least they haven't so far. In fact, they may be our only hope of overthrowing Styx Mori. He lives in mortal fear of them."

The captain takes time to help dock the boat. Then he turns and says, "You may stay with my family if you wish."

"I'll be whatever help I can," you say.

*Go on to the next page.*

Captain Soya looks at you with a steady gaze as if trying to assess your character. "You *can* help," he says. "Would you like to assist Dr. Haass with the killer bees? The work is *very* important and not as dangerous as it sounds. So far none of us have been stung. Or would you rather go on a mission to Earth to help the rebels capture Styx Mori? Our ally on Earth, named Z, is leader of the rebels. Most of the generals in Mori's army would like to overthrow him, but they are too frightened of him to try. Once he is captured, they will no longer be afraid to help Z restore freedom to Earth."

*If you say you'd rather work with Dr. Haass and the killer bees, turn to page 114.*

*If you'd rather go on the mission to Earth, turn to page 62.*

# 152

As you march along you can't help thinking again about the sorry state of Earth. A wave of sadness sweeps over you. Tokan must have noticed, for he falls in step alongside you.

"You are a brave rebel," he says. "You do not complain. I am happy you are on my team."

"What will I be doing on your team?"

Tokan moves his kerchief to cover his nose and mouth from the dust-laden wind. "Listen and you shall hear. Tomorrow we blast off and proceed to Earth. We shall make a secret landing in North America and meet another rebel force. There are many rebels on Earth. Our leader is named Z. If Mori can be captured, Z will be able to take control of his army and restore freedom to Earth."

You don't have the strength to talk and march at the same time, so you trudge on in silence. The future couldn't be more dangerous, but you feel better after hearing Tokan's plan. In fact, you can hardly wait to get back in space.

*Turn to page 54.*

What happened? Your head feels as if it's stuffed with wet cotton. You've never felt so stiff. What is that music waking you up? It's a march, "The Stars and Stripes Forever." Where are you? The dim light around you is getting brighter. You practically have to peel back your eyelids, they're so filled with sleep. What's this needle stuck in your arm? you wonder. You yank it out. A robot arm slaps a Band-Aid on the spot.

*Turn to page 155.*

You half-sit up in your tiny cot. WOW! You're beginning to remember: Dr. Grambling's proposition, the space-flight training, the briefings at the rocket base, the lessons in operating the computer, and most of all, the spooky feeling you had when they closed the capsule lid, locking you inside for over a thousand years!

Then the lift-off. The deepening blackness of space. The earth, a blue-white ball—North Africa showing between the clouds—shrinking into a tiny crescent suspended in space; and finally sleep, as your capsule settled into orbit halfway between Earth and Mars. . . .

*Go on to the next page*

# 156

You bolt out of your cot. It must be the year 3000!

A faint hum fills your space capsule, which, like the inside of a hollowed-out egg, has no particular roof or walls or floor.

"Good morning." A cheery voice greets you. "Welcome to the year 3000—January fourteenth, Earth date, to be exact. In case you forgot, I'm Winston, your on-board computer, and I'll be serving you until we make a safe landing. First of all, I'm happy to report that you came through hibernation in perfect shape. Secondly, all my functions are working perfectly, as are your space capsule's guidance and propulsion systems."

*Turn to page 4.*

You find life in your new village, named Nueva, is simple and pleasant. Fern roots are the main food; they taste something like sweet potatoes. There are also green nuts and berries. The people are kindly, and Egon and Esau become your good friends.

One day, after you've lived in Nueva awhile, Norie takes you aside.

"We have a symbiotic arrangement with the bees," she says. "They provide us with honey and we cultivate flowers. As the bees grow more numerous their collective intelligence increases. It's our hope that one day it will be sufficient so that they will figure out how to overthrow the tyrant Styx Mori and make Earth and Venus safe for all of us."

You're happy in your new home as you never thought you could be. The strange thing is that even though you've gone a thousand years into the future, the life you're leading is very much the way it might have been on Earth thousands of years in the past.

**The End**

# 158

You tug and pull at the door; it flies open. Below is a large dugout, shored up with fallen tree trunks. Your eyes roam over a bunk, a table and a bench, a tarpaulin, boxes filled with supplies, lanterns, radios, some empty boxes, an inflatable raft and an air canister, and two human skeletons!

You start to dash outdoors again but a scrap of paper on the table catches your eye. Something is written on it: FRUTAS ROJAS SIGNIFICAN LA MUERTE.

It looks as if many years ago Earth explorers were here and they spoke Spanish. You cover up the skeletons with the tarpaulin. You don't like looking at them!

After searching the bunker, you find no food, and since you're very hungry, you decide to have something to eat.

*If you eat some of the green nuts,
turn to page 26.*

*If you eat some of the red fruit,
turn to page 41.*

# 160

You feel clammy and weak after you hear this news. Poor Earth! Poor you!

Fighting back the panic that's clutching at your throat, you ask, "Is there any other place I can go? A planet? A space station?"

"Mars may be a possibility. Some refugees from the Democracy of Americas fled there a few hundred years ago, and their descendants may still be eking out a living on some desert oasis. But you must know Mars is a terribly cold, desolate place."

"What about Venus?"

Winston flashes the words PLEASE WAIT, but in a moment he replies. "Hundreds of years ago, the World Federation blew off Venus's cloud cover with massive nuclear blasts in an effort to cool the planet, increase its spin rate, and make it habitable. But soon afterward the earth was racked by wars, and I can't find any data about what's happened since."

"What about the moon?"

"Undeveloped," Winston answers. "You wouldn't last two minutes."

"Any other ideas?"

*Go on to the next page.*

You stare at the speaker on Winston's console, desperately hoping he will find a solution to your problem, but the minutes and then the hours pass. The silence, the loneliness, are more than you can bear. You must do something!

*If you tell Winston to take you to Mars, turn to page 3.*

*If you tell Winston to take you to Venus, turn to page 15.*

*If you tell Winston to take you to Earth, turn to page 8.*

*If you decide to go back into hibernation for a few hundred years in hopes that things will be better then, turn to page 24.*

Two weeks have passed since you arrived on Earth. You've found that Styx Mori makes everyone work for the tyrant's personal glorification. Your assignment is to join a group of youth workers helping to build a new wing on Mori's summer palace. You work ten hours a day laying bricks. The other workers tell you not to complain. They say life here is much better than in the military camps, where guards whip you and wake you up at all hours of the night.

You have no freedom, not even the freedom to remain silent. But you have courage. You'll never give in. Each day when you are forced to recite the pledge of allegiance to Styx Mori, you're thinking something else. You're thinking, Someday I'll escape. Someday Styx Mori will be vanquished and the world will be free.

**The End**

## ABOUT THE AUTHOR

EDWARD PACKARD is a graduate of Princeton University and Columbia Law School. He developed the unique storytelling approach used in the Choose Your Own Adventure series while thinking up stories for his children, Caroline, Andrea, and Wells. Mr. Packard is also the creator of Bantam's interactive series, *Escape From Tenopia* and *Escape From the Kingdom of Frome*.

## ABOUT THE ILLUSTRATOR

LESLIE MORRILL is a designer and illustrator whose work has won him numerous awards. He has illustrated over thirty books for children, including the Bantam Classic edition of *The Wind in the Willows*. Mr. Morrill has illustrated *Indian Trail, Attack of the Monster Plants, The Owl Tree, Sand Castle*, in the Skylark Choose Your Own Adventure series, and *Lost on the Amazon* and *Mountain Survival* in the Choose Your Own Adventure series. A graduate of the Boston Museum School of Fine Arts, Mr. Morrill lives near Boston, Massachusetts.

# CHOOSE YOUR OWN ADVENTURE®

**Prices and availability subject to change without notice.**

- - - - - - - - - - - - - - - - - - - - - - - - - - - - - - - - - - - - - - -

# BLAST INTO
# THE PAST!

# TIME MACHINE

Each of these books is a time machine and you are at the controls . . .

| | | | |
|---|---|---|---|
| ☐ | 26960 | **SECRETS OF THE KNIGHTS** #1 Jim Gasperini | $2.50 |
| ☐ | 27154 | **SEARCH FOR DINOSAURS** #2 D. Bischoff | $2.50 |
| ☐ | 26427 | **SWORD OF THE SAMURAI** #3 M. Reaves & S. Perry | $2.50 |
| ☐ | 26497 | **SAIL WITH PIRATES** #4 Jim Gasperini | $2.50 |
| ☐ | 25606 | **CIVIL WAR SECRET AGENT** #5 Steve Perry | $2.25 |
| ☐ | 25797 | **THE RINGS OF SATURN** #6 Arthur B. Cover | $2.25 |
| ☐ | 27049 | **ICE AGE EXPLORER** #7 Dougal Dixon | $2.50 |
| ☐ | 25073 | **THE MYSTERY OF ATLANTIS** #8 Jim Gasperini | $2.25 |
| ☐ | 25180 | **WILD WEST RIDER** #9 Stephen Overholser | $2.25 |
| ☐ | 26773 | **AMERICAN REVOLUTION** #10 Arthur Byron | $2.50 |
| ☐ | 26962 | **MISSION TO WORLD WAR II** #11 S. Nanus & M. Kornblatt | $2.50 |
| ☐ | 25538 | **SEARCH FOR THE NILE** #12 Robert W. Walker | $2.25 |
| ☐ | 25729 | **SECRET OF ROYAL TREASURE** #13 Carol Gaskin | $2.50 |
| ☐ | 26038 | **BLADE OF GUILLOTINE** #14 Arthur B. Cover | $2.50 |
| ☐ | 26160 | **FLAME OF THE INQUISITION** #15 Marc Kornblatt | $2.50 |
| ☐ | 26295 | **QUEST FOR THE CITIES OF GOLD** #16 Richard Glatzer | $2.50 |
| ☐ | 26421 | **SCOTLAND YARD DETECTIVE** #17 Seymour V. Reit | $2.50 |
| ☐ | 26531 | **SWORD OF CAESAR** #18 Robin & Bruce Stevenson | $2.50 |
| ☐ | 26674 | **DEATH MASK OF PANCHO VILLA** #19 G. Guthridge & C. Gaskin | $2.50 |
| ☐ | 26793 | **BOUND FOR AUSTRALIA** #20 Nancy Bailey | $2.50 |
| ☐ | 26906 | **CARAVAN TO CHINA** #21 | $2.50 |
| ☐ | 27007 | **LAST OF THE DINOSAURS** #22 | $2.50 |

**Prices and availability subject to change without notice.**

Buy them at your local bookstore or use this page to order.

- - - - - - - - - - - - - - - - - - - - - - - - - - - - - - - - -

Bantam Books, Dept. TM, 414 East Golf Road, Des Plaines, IL 60016

Please send me the books I have checked above. I am enclosing $_____
(please add $2.00 to cover postage and handling). Send check or money order
—no cash or C.O.D.s please.

Mr/Ms _____

Address _____

City/State _____ Zip _____

TM—6/88

Please allow four to six weeks for delivery. This offer expires 12/88.